{INTRODUCTION}

Hi. My name is Keesha. I am one of the kids in Ms. Frizzle's class.

Perhaps you have heard of Ms. Frizzle. (Sometimes we just call her the Friz.) She is a terrific teacher, but strange. One of her favorite subjects is science, and she knows *everything* about it.

She takes us on lots of field trips in the Magic School Bus. Believe me, it's not called *magic* for nothing! We never know what's going to happen when we get on that bus.

Ms. Frizzle likes to surprise us, but we can usually tell when she is planning a special lesson. We just look at what she's wearing.

One day Ms. Frizzle came to school wearing this outfit. One look at those lightning bolts and I knew we were going to get a big *charge* out of our next field trip! Let me tell you what happened. . . .

CHAPTER 1

"I sure wish it would rain," Phoebe said.

"You said it. The grass in the school yard could definitely use a drink," said Dorothy Ann. "It looks so dry."

Our whole class was outside. We were working on the chart we had been keeping as part of our study unit on weather. When we started a few weeks earlier, the grass was lush and green. Now it was so brown and crunchy, just looking at it made me thirsty!

"I like sunny weather, but this is too much of a good thing!" said Ralphie. He took off his baseball cap and wiped his sweaty forehead.

"How long has it been since the last time it rained, Keesha?" he asked me.

I looked at our weather chart. "Twenty-three days and counting," I told him. "There's not a cloud in the sky again today."

"Not to mention that it's hot!" Wanda said, fanning her face. "All the plants and trees are really in trouble. When are we going to get a little rain around here?"

"Excellent question!" Ms. Frizzle said.

"Today we happen to be going to the perfect place to get some answers. Is everyone ready for our trip to visit the meteorologist at the Channel Six weather center?"

"Yes!" we all answered.

All of us except Arnold, that is.

"I'm *never* ready for the Friz's field trips," he groaned.

Okay, maybe he had a point. Field trips with Ms. Frizzle on the Magic School Bus *do* tend to be filled with surprises. We can never seem to get where we're going without some kind of crazy detour!

What Is Weather?
by Keesha

Weather is the condition of the air at a particular time and place. The weather can be dry or humid, windy or calm, hot or cold, sunny or cloudy.

But you know what? It looked like this trip might be different. We all piled into the bus, and ten minutes later Ms. Frizzle pulled into the parking lot of the Channel 6 news station. We actually made it there without *anything* out of the ordinary happening.

"A normal field trip?" Tim said as we got off the bus. "Now that *is* unusual."

The Channel 6 news station was a brick building that stood on top of a hill. Two huge antennae stuck up from the roof. Not that we spent much time looking at the outside of the news station. We were more interested in checking out all the cool weather equipment *inside*.

"Let's *breeze* on in and see the professionals at work," said Carlos.

"Carlos," we all groaned.

"Follow me, future meteorologists!" Ms. Frizzle said.

We headed for the entrance. Before we could get inside, the door to the news station banged open. A young man stormed out waving a videocassette.

A meteorologist is a scientist who studies and predicts the weather.

"How can they say I'm not qualified to be a weather forecaster?" he asked. "Me, Charlie Nimbus! I said we were going to have thunderstorms, and the studio executives just laughed at me!"

Thunderstorms? We all stared up at the cloudless blue sky. I wouldn't have minded some rain. But the only stormy thing in sight was Charlie Nimbus's face!

"Thunderstorms *do* seem kind of unlikely," said Wanda.

Charlie Nimbus didn't give any sign that he'd heard her. "My hair *was* a little frizzier than usual," he said. "Except for that, my camera test was perfect! I wore my lucky tie and everything."

"Um, Mr. Nimbus? There's more to being

a weather forecaster than just looking good on camera," D.A. said.

Charlie stared at her blankly. "There is?"

I held up our class weather chart, which I had brought along on our field trip. "You have to keep track of the clouds, temperature, wind direction, and lots of other stuff," I said.

"Shouldn't you know that already, Mr. Nimbus?" Phoebe added. "I mean, you're a professional meteorologist, right?"

Charlie gave a sheepish smile. "I dropped out of meteorology class when I had the chance to star in a toothpaste commercial," he said, showing two rows of sparkling white teeth. "I guess I still have a few things to learn about weather, huh?"

Ms. Frizzle's face lit up like a 100-watt bulb. "You're in luck, Mr. Nimbus," she said. "Back on the bus, everyone. We're going to take chances! Get atmospheric! And learn about the weather!"

"Now?" I stared longingly at the Channel 6 news station. We were so close!

The Friz just herded us back onto the

bus and got behind the wheel. Charlie Nimbus sat next to Liz on the seat behind Ms. Frizzle. The first thing he did was check his reflection in the rearview mirror.

"Hmm. My hair is frizzing up even more," he said. "I'm *sure* we're going to have thunderstorms. My hair always does this when it's going to rain."

Had I heard right? Charlie Nimbus was predicting weather based on his *hair*? That didn't sound like a very scientific approach to me. Besides, the sky was totally clear.

But do you know what? Ms. Frizzle actually agreed with him!

"Thunder and lightning certainly are in the air, Mr. Nimbus," she said. "And we have front-row seats for the prestorm show."

Arnold gulped. "I don't like the sound of that."

He wasn't the only one. Every single kid on the Magic School Bus looked nervous. But did that stop the Friz? No way!

Ms. Frizzle hit the gas, and the Magic School Bus screeched out of the parking lot.

The next thing we knew, the front of the bus tilted up. It grew airplane wings and shot into the air over the Channel 6 news station.

"So much for a normal field trip," said Tim. "We're off!"

{CHAPTER 2}

The Magic School Bus zoomed through the air. Everything around us started to look bigger. Then I realized *we* were the ones changing. The bus — with us inside — was getting tinier by the second. Before long, we were so small that particles of dust looked like huge boulders floating around us.

"I never saw anything like *this* in my meteorology class," said Charlie. "W-what's happening?"

"Don't worry, Mr. Nimbus. You'll get used to the Friz's field trips," Wanda told him. "We did."

"Speak for yourself!" Arnold said. "Couldn't we just watch one of Mr. Nimbus's toothpaste commercials and forget about thunder and lightning?"

Charlie flashed those sparkling white teeth again. But not everyone noticed. Phoebe was fanning herself, and D.A. seemed to be staring off into space. I wasn't surprised to see

a book about weather — and her science notebook — on her lap. D.A. *loves* science.

"Ms. Frizzle?" D.A. said. "I have a question. You just told us thunder and lightning are in the air. Well, *I* sure don't see them."

"When it comes to the weather, you don't always have to *see* it to *believe* it," the Friz told her. "Thunderstorms start with something you can't see, even though it's in the air all around us."

Charlie turned to show us his curly locks of hair. "What about my frizzing hair? That's something you *can* see," he insisted.

"Huh?" I said. Between Charlie and Ms. Frizzle, I was totally confused!

"Thunderstorms don't start with hair, Mr. Nimbus. They start with water vapor! Water vapor is in the air," Ms. Frizzle explained. "It's something you can feel, but you can't see."

"So, *water vapor* is what makes the air feel so sticky," said D.A. While she wrote some information in her notebook, Charlie watched over her shoulder.

When Is Water a Gas?

by Tim

Water exists in the air as an invisible gas called water vapor. The sun's rays heat liquid water in rivers, lakes, and oceans. When liquid water gets hot enough, it evaporates. That means it turns into water vapor that rises and blends into the air.

"That's what's making my hair frizz up?" he asked.

"Absolutely!" Ms. Frizzle told him. She gave a tug to her own hair, which was even frizzier than usual. (Trust me, that's *very* frizzy.) "Water vapor in the air makes for stickier, sweatier, *frizzier* conditions."

"I see what you mean," said Phoebe. As she lifted her leg, it pulled away from the vinyl bus seat with a wet sucking sound. "Humid air is the reason we're in this *sticky* situation."

The air *was* starting to feel more humid. And hotter! But I still didn't understand what that had to do with a thunderstorm.

"Class, we're very lucky. We have all the ingredients for an electric storm. It's a simple recipe," said the Friz. "Start with humid air and add lots of heat from the sun. . . ."

Charlie turned his face into the bright rays that shone through the bus windows. "Phew!" He wiped his forehead. "The heat from the sun reminds me of the big lights they used when they filmed my commercial. I'm starting to sweat."

He wasn't the only one. We were all sweating like crazy!

"That's the power of the sun," Ms. Frizzle explained. "The sun is making the air hotter, too. And when air heats up, it gets lighter and rises."

"So, you're saying hot air is on the move," Carlos said with a laugh.

From D.A.'s Notebook
The Sun Gives Us Energy

Energy is what makes things move or change.

The sun provides our planet with tremendous amounts of energy. The sun's heat and light make Earth and the air around it heat up. And when the sun isn't out, things cool down. These changes cause many different kinds of weather.

From the Desk of Ms. Frizzle

Atoms on the Rise

Atoms are like tiny building blocks that are far too small to see. Everything we know is made up of atoms, including air. Heat makes atoms move faster. They bounce farther apart, so there are fewer atoms in the same amount of air. Lighter objects rise over heavier ones, so when air heats up, it rises above cooler, heavier air.

atoms in hot air

atoms in cold air

"It's no joke that hot air gets around just fine — even *without* engine power," Ms. Frizzle said. "Let's see how it's done!"

Then Ms. Frizzle did something I could *not* believe. She turned off the engine of the Magic School Bus — while we were in midair!

Ms. Frizzle could be unpredictable. I was used to that. But this seemed absolutely dangerous! I rushed to the front of the bus. I wanted to stop her, but I was too late. I gaped out the window at the hulking dust particles in the air all around the Magic School Bus. Our bus was so small, even tiny dust looked huge. We were so high up, it would be a long way to fall.

"This isn't a recipe for a thunderstorm. It's a recipe for disaster!" Carlos yelled.

I shut my eyes and waited for the Magic School Bus to plummet to the ground.

Then I heard Charlie say, "Hey! We're still rising."

Going Up!
by Phoebe

The sun heats the earth and makes the air near the surface hot. When this air rises, it makes warm gusts of air called updrafts. Thanks to updrafts, water vapor that evaporates from lakes and oceans travels high into the sky where it forms clouds.

My eyes popped open again. He was right! The bus *wasn't* falling. It kept on rising!

"I guess being full of hot air is one way of moving up in the world, or at least in the atmosphere," said Carlos.

"We're moving up, all right," said Ralphie. "But . . ." He looked around curiously. "Where are the thunderclouds?"

I still wondered about that myself. So far, we hadn't seen any dark, churning storm clouds. In fact, we hadn't seen any clouds at all!

"Maybe I can get a better look," said Charlie.

I had to hand it to him. He sure was eager to learn what made thunderstorms happen.

Maybe a little *too* eager.

Charlie climbed up on his seat and leaned way out the window. It didn't exactly look safe, especially since the air was rising faster each minute.

"Mr. Nimbus, be careful!" Wanda said.

"Wow!" he exclaimed. I thought maybe he'd spotted a thundercloud. Then I realized that wasn't it at all. Charlie was looking at his reflection in the side mirror outside the bus! He leaned even farther out the window. He even let go of the window to rub at a spot on the mirror.

"Hold on!" I yelled. "You're going to —"

I didn't have a chance to finish. At that very moment, a sudden burst of rising air lifted Charlie the rest of the way out the window.

"Help!" he shouted as he rose upward.

"We never blew people off at my old school," said Phoebe.

What could we do? We all watched helplessly as Charlie landed on an enormous particle of dust outside the bus. The dust was lifted higher and higher. The warm air carried the dust, and Charlie, straight up, up, up, and away.

{CHAPTER 3}

"We've got to help him!" said Tim.

Ms. Frizzle turned the key in the ignition. The engine chugged and sputtered but didn't start.

"Great. We've got engine trouble," Arnold groaned. "We'll never catch up to him!"

I looked up. The particle of dust with Charlie on it was just a tiny speck far above us. It rose farther away from us every second!

Then we heard a loud clank and a low growl.

"Yes!" Ms. Frizzle crowed as the engine finally started. "Not to worry, class," she assured us. "Don't forget, warm air is carrying *us* up, too. And now we've got turbo power!"

The Friz hit the gas, and the Magic School Bus flew upward even faster.

We caught up with Charlie in a flash. He was still clinging to the dust particle, and he looked terrified! But you know what? I noticed a definite spark of curiosity in his eyes, too.

The Friz brought the Magic School Bus in for a landing on the dust, and Charlie scrambled back on board.

"No clouds in sight yet," he reported. "But updrafts really gave this dust a lift! I noticed something else, too," he went on. It looked like Charlie was finally starting to pay attention. "There's a little chill in the —"

At that moment, the dust particle we were on gave a sudden lurch upward.

"Oh!" I cried.

"W-what's happening?" Arnold asked.

The Friz grinned from ear to ear. "How marvelous! Class, we just hit a cold front," she announced. "Just in case, you should all shut your windows."

Cold Fronts Are Pushy
by Keesha

A front is the boundary between two masses of air that have different temperatures and humidity. Since cold air is heavier than warm air, it pushes warm air up and out of the way.

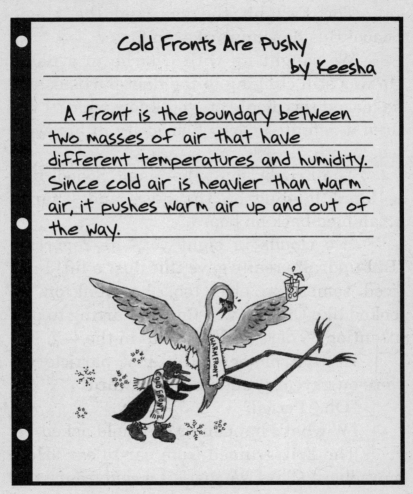

Hearing that didn't make me feel any better. Now the dust particle — with us on it — zoomed upward even faster!

"The wind is coming from the northwest," I said, glancing at the notation I had made on our weather chart. "Is that what brought the cold air our way?"

"You get the drift, Keesha!" Ms. Frizzle told me. "When that cold front pushes into our warm air, it makes the warm air move even faster. That can cause storm clouds and rain to form."

"But, Ms. Frizzle . . ." I began. I was tired of *hearing* about storms without being able to *see* them.

I guess I wasn't the only one, because everyone else chimed in:

"WHERE ARE THE THUNDER-CLOUDS?!"

At that exact moment, something amazing happened. Droplets of water appeared in the air nearby. No, scratch that. Those droplets weren't just near us. One wet bubble

formed right *around* the Magic School Bus! I sure was glad the windows were shut.

"That water appeared out of thin air!" said Ralphie. "Like magic."

"Not magic, Ralphie. Just the miracle of science in action," Ms. Frizzle said. "Class, we are now witnessing the formation of a cloud."

"*This* is a cloud?" Charlie's mouth dropped open. "I thought it was some kind of gigantic water balloon that was holding us prisoner."

For once, I understood exactly what he was talking about. All I saw was water, water everywhere!

"Water droplets may seem big when you're as tiny as we are," Ms. Frizzle explained, "but when you're a little bigger . . ."

The Friz pressed a button on the dashboard, and the Magic School Bus grew larger.

Pop!

The bus burst out of the water droplet. Now that we were bigger, I could see *millions* of tiny water droplets suspended in the air around us. They formed a light-gray haze that completely surrounded us.

"Wow. This *is* a cloud," Wanda said. "And we're right in the middle of it."

It's a Cloud!

by D.A.

The higher you travel in the atmosphere, the cooler the air is. (Warm air rises, but it becomes cooler as it moves away from the sun-heated earth. It continues to rise because it is still warmer than the surrounding air.) Cooler air makes water vapor cool down, too. Eventually, it cools enough to condense into a liquid. Tiny water droplets group together to make (you guessed it) clouds! When you see a cloud, you are really looking at millions of water droplets.

"You bet!" Ms. Frizzle pulled a poster from the glove compartment and held it up.

"Let's see. . . ." Charlie looked out the bus windows, then stared at Ms. Frizzle's chart. "The cloud we're in is fluffy and round, with a flat base," he said. All of a sudden, he snapped his fingers. "It's a cumulus cloud!" he announced.

Clouds, Clouds, Clouds!

Cumulus clouds are puffy and rounded, and cottony white. They are often seen on dry, sunny days.

cumulus

Stratus clouds form a sheetlike layer across the sky. Stratus clouds may produce a light rain, drizzle, or snow. But when they do, they get a new name: nimbostratus.

stratus

Cirrus clouds form very high in the sky, usually above 20,000 feet (6,096 m). They are made of ice crystals and have a wispy, feathery look.

cirrus

Cumulonimbus clouds are like massive cumulus clouds that can reach to great heights. They have flat tops that give them an anvil shape. Cumulonimbus clouds usually produce heavy rain, thunder, and lightning.

Cumulonimbus

"But . . . cumulus clouds form in good weather," I said, "not in thunderstorms."

"Clouds change all the time, class, just like the weather," Ms. Frizzle told us. "And this one is changing fast."

More changes? We had already been carried up in the atmosphere on hot air and totally surrounded by the tiny water droplets of a cloud. What could be next?

Like it or not, we were about to find out.

How Tiny Is That Droplet?
by Phoebe

Water droplets in clouds are 5 to 400 times smaller than the raindrops we see falling from the sky. They are tiny enough and light enough to be held aloft by warm air moving up in the atmosphere.

When droplets of water become too big and heavy to be held up they fall as rain.

CHAPTER 4

The bus began to whip around inside the cloud. It was flipping all around!

"So *this* is what it's like to have our heads in the clouds," said Carlos.

"Our heads, and the rest of us, too," said Arnold. "I can't tell which way is up!"

Neither could I. The wind inside that cloud was strong! The tiny water droplets that formed our cloud were churning around — and so were we.

"Winds have their ways of moving water droplets around inside clouds," Ms. Frizzle told us. "And that can make a cloud change in a hurry."

Taking Sides
by Ralphie

Air inside developing thunderclouds moves in a pattern. Updrafts of warm expanding air rise up on one side of the cloud. We call this the updraft side of the cloud. As the air cools, it gets heavier and moves down the other side of the cloud. That is the downdraft side of the cloud.

Wind pushed the churning water droplets of the cloud higher every second. The Magic School Bus flew up and down. Arnold was holding his arms over his stomach — trying to stop it from flipping.

"Does this bus come equipped with motion sickness bags?" he asked.

Water droplets collided all around us, forming bigger and bigger drops. Before we knew it, plenty of droplets were large enough and heavy enough to fall from the cloud as rain.

"I don't see any lightning yet, but this is *definitely* starting to feel like a storm!" said Ralphie.

This was good news for the drought — and bad, bad news for us. At least, that's what *I* thought. But Charlie was grinning from ear to ear.

"I *knew* it was going to storm," he said. He looked over his shoulder at D.A.'s notebook. "Now I know *why*. The water vapor that makes my hair frizz moves up into the atmosphere with the hot air." He snapped his fingers. "The next thing you know, there's a storm cloud."

"Actually, this air doesn't feel so hot anymore," I said, rubbing my arms. "Who turned on the air-conditioning?"

"Mother Nature did!" Ms. Frizzle answered.

Charlie looked really confused to hear that. "I don't remember learning anything about her in my meteorology class," he said.

"I thought our cloud was moving up because the air around us is *warm*," Tim added.

"It is," D.A. told him. She showed him a page in her weather book. "But the air *outside* our cloud gets cooler as we travel higher in the atmosphere. Sooner or later, the air inside the cloud cools down, too."

"Right you are, D.A.," said Ms. Frizzle. "The winds inside our cloud have stretched the cloud up so high that the air temperature at the top of the cloud is below freezing."

The goose bumps on my arms told me she was right. So did the ice crystals I saw forming in the cool air outside the bus. Now water droplets *and* ice crystals flew all around us inside that cloud. They were like high-speed bumper cars that slammed into one another.

In no time at all, the Magic School Bus was covered with water all over again. Then we banged into an ice crystal and . . .

"Hey! We froze right onto the surface of the ice," said Tim.

"We're definitely *not* a calm, puffy cumulus cloud anymore," Wanda said. "Not with all this rain, hail, and crazy wind!"

Presto Change-o . . . It's Hail!
by Tim

Hail forms when an ice crystal bumps into very cold droplets of water. The water freezes onto the surface of the ice, coating it with new layers of ice. More and more layers of ice form. Eventually the hail becomes too heavy and it falls.

No kidding! In no time at all, our cloud had blown to a huge, towering shape. The wind was so strong it swept the top of the cloud flat.

Taking a look at Ms. Frizzle's cloud chart, I realized exactly what kind of cloud we had become. We were a cumulonimbus cloud!

Mother Nature Grows Big and Tall
by Phoebe

Did you know that cumulonimbus clouds can reach heights of more than 50,000 feet? That's more than 9 miles (15 km) high!

Hailstones are usually about $2/10$-$4/10$ inch (5 to 10 mm) in diameter, but hailstones as large as $5\frac{1}{2}$ inches (140 mm) across have been seen.

Whoa! Carlos grabbed onto the seat in front of him as the bus lurched on a strong updraft. "Ms. Frizzle, I'm feeling all shook up," he said.

Ms. Frizzle's eyes sparkled. "When ice crystals and water droplets collide inside thunderclouds, they do a lot more than just shake things up. They provide just the right ingredients for thunder and lightning to make an *electrifying* entrance."

"We TV personalities know how impor-

tant it is to make a good first impression," Charlie said. Then he gave Ms. Frizzle a sheepish grin and added, "I guess you're talking about a different kind of electricity, huh?"

"You're catching my drift, Mr. Nimbus!" said the Friz. "Class, get ready for some high-voltage action. Things are about to charge up in a big way."

Clouds Change Fast!
by Tim

Winds inside a cloud — speeding upward on the updraft side, and sinking fast on the downdraft side — can change the shape of the cloud superfast. A puffy cumulus cloud can turn into a towering cumulonimbus storm cloud in as little as 30 minutes! That's not surprising, considering how fast winds can travel inside cumulonimbus clouds — more than 50 miles (80 km) per hour.

CHAPTER 5

Arnold scrunched down as far as he could in his seat. "I am *not* ready for this," he said. "Not by a long shot!"

I couldn't blame him. I was pretty nervous myself. "Did you say ch-charge up, Ms. Frizzle?" I asked.

"Sure," D.A. said. "After all, lightning is electricity, isn't it, Ms. Frizzle?"

"You said it!" the Friz told her. "When ice crystals and water droplets bump against one another in thunderclouds, a kind of energy called static electricity builds up."

"Where? Where?" Charlie asked. He

turned his head in a million different directions.

"You can't always see static electricity." D.A. handed him her notebook. "But you can read about it in my notes," she said.

Charlie started reading right away. I guess he didn't realize Ms. Frizzle's way of teaching goes a *lot* further than just getting information from books. I had started to like Charlie, and I felt sorry for him. He wanted to be a weather forecaster so badly, but he really didn't know much about weather.

"Let's find some static electricity in action, shall we?" Ms. Frizzle said.

She opened the bus door. The next thing I knew, the wind moving inside the cloud sucked us all right out of the bus!

All of a sudden, our clothes were covered by protective suits. They were kind of like the suits firefighters wear, with padding, goggles, and helmets. Not that I was complaining. The way we were blowing around inside that cloud, we really needed protection.

"We're getting smaller again," D.A. said,

holding on tight to her book about weather. "A *lot* smaller."

"Perfect!" said Ms. Frizzle. "Shrinking down to electron size is the key to learning about static electricity."

I wasn't sure what she was talking about. But I *did* know one thing. Being microscopic sure made the world look different. I didn't see water droplets and ice crystals anymore. Instead, we were surrounded by . . . To tell you the truth, I didn't know *what* to call the things I saw.

"Class, these are the atoms that make up the ice crystal we're in," Ms. Frizzle explained.

"Wow!" I said.

Those atoms were amazing! They were like balls of protons and neutrons with electrons zipping all around them. I couldn't take my eyes off them.

Then I saw a knot of protons and neutrons floating in the air on its own. Charlie noticed it, too. He stared at the protons and neutrons, frowning. Then he looked in D.A.'s notebook.

From the Desk of Ms. Frizzle

What Makes an Atom?

Atoms are made of smaller particles called protons, neutrons, and electrons. Electrons contain a negative electric charge. Protons contain a positive electric charge. Neutrons don't have any charge. The protons and neutrons group together to make the nucleus.

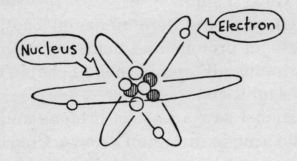

"Why doesn't that atom have any electrons?" he asked.

Before Ms. Frizzle could answer, something *really* weird happened. *We* started orbiting around the protons and neutrons.

"Whoa!" Tim said as we zipped around and around the center of the atom. "Does this mean — ?"

"*We're* the electrons!" Wanda finished.

"Right you are!" said Ms. Frizzle. "Usually, an atom contains an equal number of protons and electrons."

D.A. nodded. "According to my research, the positive charge of protons balances out the negative charge of electrons, so that the whole atom doesn't have *any* electric charge."

"So true!" Ms. Frizzle said. "But sometimes atoms bump into one another. . . ."

"Like the atoms of water droplets and ice crystals that keep crashing together inside our cumulonimbus cloud?" Ralphie said.

The Friz grinned from ear to ear. "You get the picture, Ralphie!" she said. "When atoms collide, electrons from one atom can rub off onto another atom . . . with *electric* results."

We didn't have to wait long to see for ourselves what she was talking about.

"Yikes! Incoming atoms!" Ralphie announced.

Atoms zoomed toward us from all directions.

Wham!

An atom hit us. It was part of a hail-stone. It zoomed off again in a flash — taking Wanda, Tim, and Ralphie with it.

"Oh, no!" I shouted, watching my friends orbit around with the electrons of the other atom.

"Don't look now. Here come some more!" Arnold said.

Wham! Bang!

Two more atoms smashed into us. They were part of a large raindrop. Electrons were everywhere! The two atoms bounced away fast. This time, I felt *myself* being pulled along with one of them. D.A., Phoebe, and Arnold came right along with me.

"Here we go!" D.A. said.

Looking back, I saw that Carlos and Ms. Frizzle had rubbed off onto the second atom.

"I sure get a *charge* out of being in a thundercloud," yelled Carlos.

We all groaned, "Carlos!"

This was bad. Very bad. The kids from our class were on three different atoms!

Swirling winds made atoms fly all around inside the cloud. We were lucky that the three atoms with us on them stayed together. They began to sink down in the cloud.

"Hey!" Charlie's cry rang out from above us. "What about me?"

Oops! None of us had noticed that Charlie had been left behind on our old atom. He orbited around the protons and neutrons at the atom's center. But, while our atoms were moving downward, his was moving up!

D.A. clutched her weather book and stared at Charlie. "He's got my notebook!" she said. "And he's moving farther and farther up."

Poor Charlie! Now that he wasn't with Ms. Frizzle anymore, how was he going to learn about weather?

"Why isn't Charlie's atom moving down with the rest of us?" Tim asked.

Looking up, I saw that Charlie's atom didn't have nearly as many electrons as it had had before the other atoms rammed into it. "I get it," I said. "Charlie's atom has more protons than electrons, so it's positively charged, right?"

"You said it!" Ms. Frizzle agreed. "His atom is moving to the top of the thundercloud with all the other positively charged atoms."

I looked at the three atoms around which the rest of us orbited. "So our atoms, which have more electrons, are moving down to the bottom of the cloud," I said.

"Which means we have a negative charge of static electricity!" Tim finished.

Electrons Throw Their Weight Around
by Ralphie

Electrons jump from one atom to another when water droplets, raindrops, and hailstones smash into one another. The warmest objects, like heavy raindrops and hailstones, collect the most electrons. These heavy objects fall to the lower part of the cloud, so most of the electrons are in the bottom of the cloud.

"I guess when it comes to static electricity," said Carlos, "being negative can really bring you down."

"Carlos," we all groaned again.

Carlos is the king of bad jokes. But he

was right about one thing: Our negatively charged atoms went down, down, down. Before long, we reached the bottom of the cloud.

It was really crowded down there. More and more negatively charged atoms collected around us. Electrons jostled together, and we were right in the thick of it. The feeling was . . . well, it felt *electric*!

Ralphie looked around in amazement. "So *this* is what happens when static electricity builds up!" he said.

What Makes Electricity Static?
by Phoebe

We say something is static when it doesn't change or move. Static electricity is a kind of stored energy because the electrons are relatively motionless. Static electricity cannot power appliances or release heat and light.

By now, we had totally lost sight of Charlie. It was hard to even tell which way was up with all those negatively charged atoms around us. How were we ever going to find Charlie again?

I didn't have much time to worry about that, though.

"Hey!" I gulped as I felt a kind of pressure tugging at me from below. "What's going on?"

Carlos looked around with wide eyes. "That's the megawatt question, Keesha," he said.

"Absolutely," the Friz agreed. "And we're about to learn the answer."

CHAPTER 6

The next thing I knew, electrons all around us shot down from the bottom of the cloud. And we were pulled right along with them! We zoomed toward the earth in a tube-like channel.

Bad, oh bad, oh bad, bad, bad! My heart leaped into my throat as we sped along.

"Ms. Frizzle," yelled Ralphie. "What's happening?"

"Electricity is what's happening!" Ms. Frizzle announced. "When the charge at the base of the cloud becomes strong enough, electric energy is released."

If It's Moving, It Isn't Static
by Keesha

When the electrons "held" in static electricity are pushed into motion, they create an active kind of energy called current electricity.

Electric current goes with the flow. Just as a current in a stream is a flow of water, electric current is a flow of electrons.

"You mean *we're* electric energy?" Arnold asked as we whooshed down from the cloud with the other electrons.

"You bet!" the Friz answered. "We're an electric current."

"Is that what flows through the wires in your house?" asked Tim.

"Yes, but this current is stronger — a lot stronger," said Ms. Frizzle.

"But . . . now that we know we're a current, where are we going?" Phoebe wanted to know.

"I think I can answer that," said D.A. She held up her weather book. "It says in here that the negative electric charges at the bottom of the cloud are attracted to positive charges in the ground below."

Opposites Attract
by Wanda

Opposite electric charges (positive and negative) attract each other. Electric charges that are the same (positive and positive, or negative and negative) push each other away.

Lightning Moves in Steps
by Carlos

The stream of electrons released from the bottom of a cumulonimbus cloud moves toward the ground in a series of strokes. This stream is called a "stepped leader." Each stroke lasts for just a fraction of a second, and it takes about four strokes for a stepped leader to reach the ground. That's fast!

So if what D.A. said was true, we were whizzing at lightning speed toward the ground.

"I've heard of kids being grounded," said Carlos, "but this is ridiculous!"

"Oh, why did we have to turn into electrons?" Arnold asked, groaning.

Let me tell you, we weren't just moving. We went like a streak! *Zip! Zoom! Zing!*

We zigzagged down toward the earth in strokes that followed each other so quickly I couldn't keep track of them. And every zig and zag took us farther away from Charlie Nimbus.

See That Crooked Lightning?
by D.A.

Ever wonder why lightning is so jagged? It's because a stepped leader doesn't move in a straight line. It makes a crooked, zigzag path down from the cloud.

"I see the ground!" Tim announced.

Somehow, I made myself look down. Sure enough, the leafy tops of trees were there below us. Thanks to my special goggles, I saw something else, too — a stream of positive electric charges that jumped toward us from the highest treetop.

"How marvelous!" said the Friz. "That streamer is coming up to meet us . . . right on schedule!"

Positive Charges Jump
by Arnold

As a stepped leader nears the ground, it can create a pull so strong that the positive atoms in the ground rise to meet it. This channel of positively charged atoms is called a streamer.

A streamer often forms, but not always.

"Marvelous is not exactly the word I'd use," said Arnold. "More like terrifying."

That streamer sure seemed eager to get to us. It jumped straight toward us from the top of that tree. And then . . .

"We've got contact!" cried Ms. Frizzle.

At that moment, the stepped leader and the streamer met.

I shut my eyes. This was too much. Way too much!

"Uh-oh," I heard Carlos say. "Get ready for an electrifying ride!"

Lightning You Can See
by Phoebe

When we see a bolt of lightning, we're not seeing stepped leaders and streamers. They are not visible. The lightning we see forms only after the negative stepped leader makes contact with the positive atoms in the ground.

CHAPTER 7

Everything got superbright and white hot. I was soooo glad we had those suits and goggles for protection.

"We're really getting electric now!" said Tim.

"This is it!" the Friz agreed. "Once a streamer and a stepped leader meet, they form a path between the cloud and the ground. That lets a very powerful current of electrons travel back up to the cloud. The current of electrons is so strong it releases tremendous amounts of heat and light . . ."

". . . Which we see as a bolt of lightning!" D.A. finished.

I couldn't see anything, we were moving so fast.

We zoomed back up toward the cloud with all the other electrons. At least, I think that's what was happening. With all that white-hot heat and light around us, it was hard to know for sure.

"I'm afraid to look!" said Arnold. "Tell me when —"

BOOM!

An explosion shook the air around us. Let me tell you, it was more than just loud. That noise was deafening!

"L-let me guess," Arnold said through chattering teeth. "That was thunder?"

"Right again!" Ms. Frizzle answered.

What Makes Thunder?
by Ralphie

Lightning heats up the air around it in an instant. The heat makes the air expand VERY FAST. When the hot air hits the colder air around it, it makes a big noise. That's thunder.

I shook my head until the ringing in my ears stopped. "So," I said, "lightning releases three kinds of energy — heat, light, and sound."

"I just want to know when it's going to release us," said Arnold. "I want to get out of here!"

I definitely agreed. But for Ms. Frizzle, riding a bolt of lightning was more fun than the Supersonic Whip at the amusement park.

"Wa-hoo!" she shouted.

"Class, we're moving at the speed of lightning. That's 90 thousand miles per second, in case you're wondering."

D.A. punched some numbers into her pocket calculator. "Which is equal to 100 million feet per second!" she added.

So that's why we were traveling so fast.

In a flash, we were back up at the bottom of the cloud.

Phoebe's Big Question

Q. Why do we usually hear thunder after we see lightning?

A. Because light travels faster than sound — more than 1 million times faster. That means light from a bolt of lightning reaches us almost at once. Sound travels just ⅕ mile per second, so it takes longer to get to us.

"Phew!" I said. Finally, things slowed (and cooled) down enough for us to look around.

"Hey, we're all electrons on the same atom again!" said Tim.

I guess shooting down to the earth and back again had shaken up a lot of electrons. Sure enough, we were all zipping around a single knot of protons and neutrons again. All of us except Charlie, that is. I still didn't see any sign of him. But I did see something else.

"The Magic School Bus!" I shouted.

There it was, resting among the electrons at the base of the thundercloud. Liz was at the wheel. She opened the door. But when we tried to get to the bus, we couldn't!

"The pull of our atom is holding us in orbit," D.A. said. "We can't break free."

Bad, oh bad, oh bad, bad, bad! I didn't think things could get any worse. But then they did.

Whoosh!

A strong updraft swept up our atom, sending us flying high into the cloud.

The Magic School Bus disappeared from sight far below us — again! I should have known it was just a matter of time before we started colliding with other atoms.

Wham!

"Not again," Arnold groaned.

Sure enough, we had hit another atom. One of its electrons broke free and began orbiting our atom. But it wasn't just any electron.

"Charlie Nimbus!" we all cried.

We all cheered as he zipped into orbit around our atom, still holding onto D.A.'s notebook.

"I've been reading up on static electricity and electric storms," Charlie said, waving the notebook. "Did you know that when electrons

are transferred from one atom to another inside cumulonimbus clouds, huge amounts of static electricity build up? Positive electric charges build up at the top of the cloud, and negative charges build up at the bottom."

I have to admit, I was impressed. Charlie was starting to sound as if he really knew what he was talking about!

"Actually, we found that out for ourselves when we took an electrifying ride to the ground and back on a lightning bolt," D.A. said.

"Wow!" Charlie's eyes went wide. "I think I saw a different kind of lightning," he said. "One that stayed inside the cloud. . . ."

"Wow! If it was inside the cloud, it must have been close," Wanda said.

How Far Away Is That Lightning?
Do the Numbers and Find Out!
by Wanda

First, count the seconds between the flash of lightning and the crack of thunder. Then divide by 5. The answer is the number of miles between where you are and where the lightning struck.

15 seconds divided by 5 = 3 miles away.

Arnold gulped and looked nervously around us. "You mean there's more lightning around here?" he asked.

"Oh, yes!" said the Friz. "This storm isn't done yet. The light show is just getting started!"

CHAPTER 8

Wasn't one lightning bolt enough? I sure thought so. But I guess our cloud had other ideas.

Cra-ackkk! BOOM!

A flash of lightning shot between the top of the cloud and the bottom of it.

It lit up the whole cloud. The roaring clap of thunder that followed made us all cover our ears.

"There it is again!" said Charlie. "That's the same kind of lightning I saw before."

Ralphie frowned. "That lightning didn't go anywhere near the ground," he said. "It never even left our cloud."

"Only about one out of every five lightning bolts strikes the ground," Ms. Frizzle told us. "All the rest travel from one cloud to another or between different parts of the same cloud."

Lightning: Where and When?
by Ralphie

- Lightning strikes somewhere on the earth every second.
- In the United States, lightning strikes the ground 15–20 million times a year.
- Lightning occurs more often in Florida with its warm, moist climate than anywhere else in the United States.

Ms. Frizzle reached into the zippered pocket of her protective suit. She pulled out another diagram and held it up for us to see.

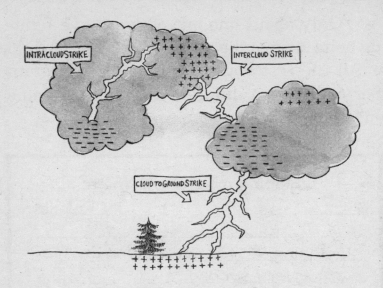

"Wow," said Carlos. "That's some pretty *striking* information."

Charlie took one look at Ms. Frizzle's chart and started to write notes in D.A.'s notebook.

"So that lightning just happens when a stepped leader travels from a negatively charged part of a cloud to a positive part of the same cloud, right?" Charlie said.

The Friz nodded. "You're really charged with weather facts now, Mr. Nimbus!" she said.

Can You Name That Lightning?
by Carlos

Sheet lightning can't be seen clearly because it is hidden by clouds. Someone watching from the ground can see the whole cloud light up.

Heat lightning is lightning that is so far away – usually farther than 10 miles (16 km) – that you can't hear its thunder.

Ball lightning is a glowing ball of lightning that can last from a few seconds to a few minutes. Ball lightning is very rare and usually occurs in violent storms that contain lots of lightning.

St. Elmo's fire appears over pointed objects on the ground, like power poles and antennae. It is a series of tiny sparks that travel from positive charges on the ground toward negatively charged pockets in the sky. This creates a bluish or greenish glow.

"But I want to know more," said Charlie. He couldn't seem to get enough! Maybe Charlie might achieve his ambition after all. As we zoomed around the center of our atom, he looked at D.A.'s weather book. "What about cloud-to-cloud lightning? And sheet lightning? Can we see them, too?"

Arnold groaned and buried his head in his hands. "With all these different kinds of lightning around, we're going to be toast!"

Lightning Hurts
by Keesha

Nine out of every 10 people struck by lightning survive the event. Even so, lightning kills nearly 100 people each year in the United States.

Lightning damages houses, buildings, and forests, too. Every year that damage costs about $2 billion!

"Lightning is dangerous, Arnold," Ms. Frizzle admitted.

"Now she tells us," said Arnold.

"But," the Friz went on, "there are ways people can keep safe in thunderstorms."

Ms. Frizzle's Tips for Staying Safe During Thunderstorms

If you are inside or can get inside:
- Stay inside.
- Don't use the phone.
- Keep away from electric appliances and outlets, plumbing fixtures, and other metal objects. Believe it or not, the metal plumbing and wiring in the walls of a house form a protective barrier. That's because lightning

travels on the surface of the metal. It can't reach objects inside the network of metal. As long as you stay inside during thunderstorms — and as long as you don't touch any metal — you will be safe.

If you are outside:

- Keep away from water.
- Take shelter in a car with a metal roof. The metal of the car will form a protective barrier. Again, stay inside the car, and be sure not to touch the metal parts of the car.

If there's no shelter:
- Crouch down on both feet in a low, dry place.

- **DO NOT TAKE SHELTER UNDER A TREE.**
Tall objects such as trees attract lightning.

I sure was glad to know how to keep safe in a thunderstorm, but we weren't exactly normal kids in a normal storm right then. We were electrons!

"Maybe there's a silver lining to this thundercloud," Carlos said. "People say that lightning never strikes the same place twice. We've already hit the ground with lightning once, so maybe we're safe."

Lightning Likes to Repeat Itself
by Arnold

If you think lightning can't strike the same place more than once, think again! Lightning hits the Empire State Building about 21 to 25 times every year. Lightning can strike the same person more than once, too. One park ranger was struck by lightning seven different times. (The good news is that he survived them all!)

D.A. turned to a page of her book about weather. "I hate to be the one to break it to you, but lightning *can* strike the same place more than once," she said.

Did I really need to hear that? No way!

"I sure would like to get away from here," I said. "Say 10 or 20 miles away."

"We'd have to go farther than that to steer clear of lightning, Keesha," Ms. Frizzle informed me. "Lightning can hit the ground as far as 40 miles away from a storm. And once it strikes, it can spread out more than 50 feet."

"So detecting and tracking storms is more than just a way for meteorologists to get on TV," said Charlie. "It's a way to help people stay safe."

"Now you're looking on the sunny side of things, Mr. Nimbus," said Ms. Frizzle.

I was glad our protective suits were keeping us safe. Winds carried us past half a dozen different bolts of lightning inside the cloud. We rammed into so many atoms, I lost count!

"This atom has gained a lot of electrons,"

Charlie commented. "Look, we're sinking down to the bottom of the cloud."

As we floated downward, I kept looking for the Magic School Bus. I had had enough of the electric life! Too bad all I saw were more and more negatively charged atoms, crowding around us. The bus was nowhere to be found.

"Yippee!" Charlie bounced and jostled against all the electrons, waving D.A.'s notebook in the air. "My meteorology teacher never told me rubbing elbows with electrons could be so exciting."

"It's electric, all —" said Tim.

But Tim didn't have a chance to finish his sentence.

Whoosh!

A stream of electrons shot down from the bottom of the thundercloud.

"It's another stepped leader!" D.A. said. "And we're part of it."

"Not again," groaned Arnold.

Not that we could do anything to stop the stepped leader from taking us with it. We zigzagged down toward the ground so fast that it was hard to see straight.

"Hey!" Tim looked down and pointed. "There's the Channel Six news station." I managed to spot the building, sitting all by itself at the top of a hill.

"Whoa!" I said, blinking. "A streamer just jumped up from that antenna on the news station roof!"

"That's a streamer, all right," the Friz agreed. "But that pole isn't an antenna. It's a lightning rod!"

Charlie flipped through D.A.'s notebook.

Lightning Rods Take the Heat Off
by D.A.

Want to know how people protect houses and businesses from lightning? They use lightning rods!

Lightning rods are made of a metal that conducts electricity, usually copper or aluminum. Rods are placed on top of a building and are connected to cables that lead to metal rods driven into the ground. Instead of striking the building, lightning flows harmlessly into the ground.

"Hmm. It says here that once a streamer makes contact with a stepped leader," Charlie said, "electrons flow superfast to make a bolt of lightning."

"Mr. Nimbus, you're showing a stroke of genius for weather," said the Friz. She didn't have time to tell Charlie any more about it. At that moment, the streamer and the stepped leader met.

"Uh-oh," I said.

Then everything went white-hot.

CHAPTER 9

"Get ready for a megawatt dose of heat, light, and sound energy!" said Carlos.

"I wasn't ready the first time. I am definitely not ready now," Arnold said.

All at once, we were surrounded by superbright light and a hot, hot, hot blast of heat. The roaring *BOOM* of thunder came, making me feel as if we would fall right out of the sky.

This was too much! All I could do was clamp my hands over my ears and close my eyes, waiting for it to end.

Then, in an instant, it was over.

The air felt cool and wet. The only sound

I heard was the heavy patter of rain and hail falling. I took a deep breath and opened my eyes.

"Hey! We're back in the parking lot of the Channel Six news station," I said.

"The Magic School Bus is here, too!" said Phoebe.

Our protective suits and goggles were gone. We were our regular size again — and so was the Magic School Bus. It was parked in the lot right next to us. Rain and hail pelted down from above, but we were so dazed, we just stood there getting wet.

Charlie shook his head and blinked a few times. He stared at the smoke that rose up from the lightning rod.

"Did we just turn into a thundercloud and zap down here on a bolt of lightning?" Charlie asked. He looked kind of confused — as if he couldn't quite believe what he had said. Maybe it was just a dream.

I didn't blame him for being puzzled. The first time I went on one of the Friz's field trips, I had a hard time believing it was real, too!

"Just look at Charlie's hair," Wanda whispered to me. "That's definite proof that he's been zapped."

She wasn't kidding, either. Charlie's hair wasn't just frizzy. It stuck straight up from the top of his head!

We all turned as the door to the news station banged open. Half a dozen people piled out of the station. They gaped at the smoking lightning rod, all talking at once.

"Wow!"

"Did you see that lightning?"

"I thought the sky was going to split open."

"That lightning made a direct hit to the lightning rod!"

They looked really worried when they saw us standing out in that storm. But Ms. Frizzle told them we were all right.

"Getting up close and personal with thunder and lightning has been a wonderfully *electric* experience," said the Friz. "Wouldn't you agree, Mr. Nimbus?"

Charlie flashed his sparkling white teeth. "Absolutely," he said. He handed D.A. her notebook and turned to the studio executives. "This thunderstorm was sudden. But, as we aspiring meteorologists know, cumulonimbus clouds can form fast — in as little as 30 minutes. . . ."

Those studio executives sure weren't laughing at Charlie now. They listened closely as he went on to talk about water vapor, cloud formation, and static electricity that builds up inside cumulonimbus clouds.

When he was done, the studio executives talked seriously among themselves. I went over to Charlie and said, "You sound like a serious weather forecaster now, Mr. Nimbus. But . . . well, you might want to fix your hair before your next camera test."

Charlie glanced at his reflection in the side mirror of the Magic School Bus.

"Having a bad hair day doesn't bother me anymore," he said. "Nice-looking hair isn't nearly as interesting as tracking and forecasting the weather."

A big smile spread across Ms. Frizzle's face. "I can see that our trip has cleared up some weather issues for you, Mr. Nimbus," she said. "From now on, I'm sure you'll be dedicated to completely accurate forecasts."

Apparently, the studio executives thought so, too. As they led Charlie back inside the studio to continue his job interview, we heard him saying, "I'm planning to go back to school and learn even more about weather. I think education is so important, don't you?"

We were right behind them. We were finally going to get our tour of the weather center!

Everyone had a great time. We even got to stand in front of the camera and see ourselves on the TV weather map. That was when I noticed that Charlie wasn't the only one

whose hair had been zapped. We all had gotten a charge from Ms. Frizzle's field trip.

Our field trip had definitely been *electrifying*. I knew we would never forget it.